Beds & Shotguns

Beds & Shotguns

Diana Fitzgerald Bryden
Paul Howell McCafferty
Tricia Postle
Death Waits

edited and designed by Mike O'Connor

INSOMNIAC PRESS

Copyright © 1995 Insomniac Press
All rights reserved.

editor
Mike O'Connor

copy editors
Phlip Arima
Lloyd Davis
Waheeda Harris

Canadian Cataloguing in Publication Data

Main entry under title:

Beds and shotguns

Poems.
ISBN 1-895837-28-6

1. Canadian poetry (English) - 20th century.*
I. O'Connor, Mike, 1968-

PS8293.B43 1995   C811'.54.5408   C95-930199-2
PR9195.7.B43 1995

Printed and bound in Canada.

Insomniac Press
378 Delaware Ave.
Toronto, Ontario, Canada
M6H 2T8

Diana Fitzgerald Bryden's *Song for a Dead Actor* first appeared in *Shift Magazine* and *Theft* was the title poem from a self-published chapbook.

If It's Worth Going Out,
It's Worth Dressing Up
Tricia Postle
7

Only a Profound Thought Can Spawn a Demon
Death Waits
29

10,000 Leagues Under the Skull
Paul Howell McCafferty
51

A Home So Far It's Nowhere But Memory
Diana Fitzgerald Bryden
73

if it's worth going out, it's worth dressing up

tricia postle

memory

I keep most of it
Behind this false backing,
    here,
There's a few things cluttered,
If you step carefully
Over the packing crate;
I've got my great
Grandmother's china cups
Just bear with me, I'll
Put on some tea, switch
On a light, and
    there!

I've got copies of Ventadorn,
Assorted Romances and the Voir Dit,
Gut strings, some photos,
Grave rubbings, and an exaggeratedly
Flattering portrait of Oscar Wilde,
A miniature of Sir Walter Raleigh,
My grandmother's eyes, and
The family history.
The blouse my mother made
When I was six, and these little
Plastic figurines got in here,
Somehow, and I never threw them out.

And if you look inside that box,
    there,
I think you'll see the
Stoop of your shoulders and
Your hands, cradling
A cup of coffee.
I've been housecleaning, but
I hate to throw things out.

amor i

I've finally received
My severance pay,
Vacation pay, and
Compensation for injuries
Suffered in the workplace
From my last deity,
Being Amor, Love's
Personification and
Ruler of Love's court.

These days I'm only
Doing freelancing,
And it pays much better.

amor ii

This is a love song,
This is really a love song,
Though if you played it backward
In a fit of sudden suspicion
You might find some subliminal messages.

But really this is a love song,
This is really a love song,
Though if in a fit of erudition,
You gave it a deconstructionalist reading
It might prove less than certain,
For nothing is really certain,
But this is a love song.

amor iii

Love is a card, and should be dealt with.
Love gave me his business card,
But he didn't say which company
He's working for.

Love gave me his business card,
And I feel flattered;
He wrote his home number on the back.
But he's never home, and when he is
There's a woman's voice in the background.
He claims it's Psyche, but you know,
One can't be too careful.
Love gave me a bunch of idiosyncratic messages
That leave me with nothing to assume.

I called Love at work and his secretary answered
(A male secretary, but I've suspected
That Love is bi for a while now.)
I asked for the company name
He answered: socioeconomic imperative.
I called again later that afternoon
The same secretary told me that
The company was named self-actualization.

I called fifteen minutes later.
A woman told me
That I had reached the Personal Insurance Co.
And that Love didn't work there any more.

sweet breath at night

There are panthers in my bedroom
Flame-eyed with waving tails;
Bright burning eyes with
Harsh sandpaper tongues;
Coal-eyed panthers, more and less,
With tongues like glass.

I plan to be eccentric, old
With a hundred cats;
But panthers are madness,
I must be off my bat;
I'm not old enough to be harmless,
Not yet.

They sheathe their claws
And wander as they will,
Drinking from the toilet bowl,
And fading through the walls;
But one sits by me,
Growling or purring,
Sitting, staring, still;
Glaring through committed eyes.

Until I'm not sure who's burning,
Not sure who's sleeping,
Not sure whose claws are where.

bestiary

Here's a lion:
His back is like a monkey's;
His tail is like a snake;
His mane is like an actor's wig.
He signifies lust;
You can tell by the way
He moves across the page, intent.
He has this property:
With every breath he becomes darker
Until he's entirely obscured,
Slipping through the night like a dream.

Here's a nightingale,
With bloody feathers like a hawk's lure,
A tiny body that fluttered like a dancer in black rags,
Like a book with black pages.
I send his body to you as a love token,
Still warm.
If you press
His tiny bloodstained throat to your ear,
You may still hear singing.

Some might send flowers,
But I'm sending a bestiary;
Dried and pressed animals
That squirm in my arms like children.

A cock and a hen,
In memory of a child
Hung out on a hemp rope
To twist in the wind.
See the scars under his wing
From my knife and fork,
Roasted, they started to fly and squawk and crow.
The child, cut down,
Came back to life.

And here's a unicorn,
With a goat's tail and heart.
I spearpointed him, drove him
Between gates, fenced him
Under the pomegranate like some
Exotic beast. He obliged,
Looking stranger every day,
Until he changed into a hand mirror.

There you are,
Painted Limbourg blue and gold like an angel,
Every curve compressed into a flat surface,
And a circle of nothingness around your body.

commedia dell'arte

This poem is based on characters from the commedia dell'arte, an improvised Italian renaissance comedy that ran from pathos to slapstick. This poem is fondly dedicated to I Sebastiani, the Greatest Comedia dell' Arte Troupe in the Entire World.

1.
This pervasive melancholy
Crystalline tears shed
This mask I play
As with artistry and grace
The latest theatrical achievement
(Watch carefully)
I die for love.

2.
Dear sir, I pray you,
Be gentle to yourself
As I return your letters,
Unopened,
With consummate poise;
My skirts gathered
I retreat offstage.

3.
This immoderate amatory influence
(Amax Superfliicistis in the Latin)
Is caused by an imbalance of the sanguine humours
Resulting from an unfavourable conjunction
Of Venus, Mars and my pocketbook.
This plethoric individual
Must constrain his impetuosity
And seek immediate medical attention.

4.
Nay! Cease, thou Base-born Knave, unworthy
Rogue! Darken no more the path of that
Fair Image of Venus, or face the Wrath of the
Terrible Captain Blunderbuss, Decapitator of
Dozens, Slayer of Scores, and Terror of the
World Entire!
Oh!
        pray pardon i was once near eaten by the
        notorious giant rats of partha and have since
        morbidly feared mice pray madam call thy cat!

5.
Fair sir, I fear
I love thee not a whit
More than before, and as
For this pretty bagatelle, what
Of it? I flutter my fan
And step modestly back into darkness.

6.
(I trust
Your attention is not slipping? Good.)
So here I am left
To languish in sorrow and regret:
Watch!
The distant, sightless gaze of a forlorn man
As I stagger back, sink down
And my lips murmur one last time her sweet name
As I collapse to thunderous applause.
Goodnight!

7.
(Harlequin enters. Rude gestures,
Cartwheels. Exit.)

bounce

Swinging to love,
Swinging to loss,
It's a trampoline;
Rattling like a glass eye
In a truffle box.
When we kiss,
Light springs
Out of your mouth,
Leaps behind my eyes.

A small round man
With glasses blows the blues
Out of his lips,
Like a pet budgie
Perched in front of the mirror.
I look into your eyes
And see someone else;
Who's swinging now?

I've noted something low
About the bounce of sound:
A sine-wave shift
You stand, arms
Looped out to either side
Knocking the aggie out of the circle
With a sweet taste.

A part of me
Is lost when you're not here,
And a larger part
Falls out when you're around,
Who's swinging now?

Hanging on a word,
Then letting go and dropping
To the ground.
Trampolined again,
Shoes in the clouds:
There was an I somewhere
But half a beat behind;
It's a jazz motion,
And I'm swinging again.

L'Envoi/Oh Boy:

Cats and catesses,
Poet and poetrix,
Tripping the energy
Matter constant:
Old light switch,
New tricks.
There was an eye somewhere,
But half a beat behind;
It's a jazz E-motion,
And I'm swinging again.

festival

Long wind-y train down south,
Eating hobo stew with a harmonica.
Then down to Orleans,
Kiss my Mardi Gras.

Festival,
Festival,
Festival.

Alright, you feet;
Lazy day up till now.
Now in this afternoon,
Start dancing all night through.
Long wind-y train!
Feet dancing all night through!

Festival,
Festival,
Festival.

Why these hips dancing,
Shaking all night through,
Dancing all night through?
If you wag your tongue at me,
I'll wag my hips at you.
Alright, you hips,
Lazy day until now.
Now in this afternoon,
Start dancing all night through.
Long wind-y train!
Feet dancing all night through!
Hips shaking all night through!

Festival,
Festival,
Festival.

Don't want to be a slave to be free;
Don't want to be free to be a slave.
I want to dance all night through,
I want to dance all night through.

Alright, you feet,
Lazy day until now.
Now in this afternoon,
Start dancing all night through.

Long wind-y train!
Feet dancing all night through!
Hips shaking all night through!
Up and down here all night through.
In and out the whole night through.
Round and round the whole night through.
In and out the whole night through.
Front and back the whole night through.
Inside outside whole night through.
Circle round the whole night through.
Upside down the whole night through.

Long wind-y train!
Feet dancing all night through!
Hips shaking all night through!

Festival,
Festival,
Festival.

roses breathing / roses burning

Sacred art
Your eyes are turning
In again
The all-divining
All-discerning
Nothing comes to you like roses breathing
Roses burning

Oh your eyes
They are the night
Lit shadows keep me in
I cannot keep the thought
Of your reclining
From my mind which clings
You break the night
With thought that sings
Where others whisper
From the breaking of the light
You catch the fire
Your eyes are lit
And all is empty with the thought
Of roses breathing
Roses burning

ave gratia plena

Noel, Noel,
Noel, Noel:
This is the salutation
Of the angel Gabriel.

In te, Domine, speravi.
Leave me, you
Unfocused thoughts;
Herbs dried in bunches,
Heal my mind;
In te, Domine, spero.

Light patterns
The wood table;
I would rise,
But am held,
The words ringing
Through me:
Ave fitt ex Eva.

Loose-draped
Levite cloth,
Wrought iron,
Extinguished candle;
I am transfigured,
While the lights are out.
Manifest love
Flies in and whispers;
I submit,
Love compels me.
Ecce ancilla Domine.

The words are clear,
My mind is clear;
The candle is inside me,
Shining out,
Calling with clear
Annunciation:
Nova, Nova.

Noel, Noel,
Noel, Noel:
This is the salutation
Of the angel Gabriel.

brine

There is an ocean here,
That's breaking, flooding, ready to uprise;
The tide is higher every minute,
And every grain of sand cries out:

Here is the end of the line,
Here is a faith without end,
For we have waited all winter,
And now we are clean again;

Here is Gabriel, and his horn
Can be heard in the crash of the sea,
Line up, starfish and oysters!
Here is the judgment day.

The conch-shell trumpet sounding clear
Lifts up our eyes to beaches where
Our kelp is lying. I'm afraid
The loafing fishes do not hear.

fury

I'm an evangelist, my tongue is on fire
Burning my mouth,
I pull out words with a stage flourish
Yes, these came from a heart that knows
Something about temperature.
And what am I talking about?
You, your searing glance, and your catch-phrase mouth
You and that serpent staff
And the woman you threw down.
You've got a hat full of sparkling dust
That tastes like ashes. Marvellous, what expertise,
You fill the room with smoke.
What then? On a hunch
I wait. Expectant pause, but
Nothing new comes out from under that hat of yours
Unless someone else speaks first.
I catch your eye with your secret, you
Open your mouth as if to make a sound,
But before a word creeps out you've shrunk
Into a cinder.

revelation in transit

No one looks comfortable at Kipling station,
Not at this hour;
Lacquered women eating crackers,
Sticky children being hauled
Like sacks of grain, complaining loudly,
To their father standing grimly
Looking at his watch, face pained.

The bus curbed like a whale
Prophetess in a coral necklace
Disembarks and Are we saved?
It's too early. All your apocalypses
Can wait at least till noon.
But now I've got a tract
That tells me, if I sign
My name right there then I will join
The company of the Elect.
Yes, some of us will catch the bus
Some won't.

today i'm going to be a man

Today, I'm going to be a man.
I'm going to wear black clothes
And no makeup.
OK.   No difference.
But it's inside
I'm wearing black clothes
And no makeup
And I won't think
That I'd look better with eyeliner.
Today, I'm a man.
I'm not going to wear any fitted clothing.
If someone wants
To know that I have breasts,
They're going to have to look.
I'm wearing a black suit jacket.
I'm a man.

Today, I'm going to be a man.
I have short hair, and a
Black suit jacket, and
I'm six feet tall;
Today, I'm a man.
I'm saying just what's on my mind,
Even if it's not much.
I'm a man!

Today, I'm going to be a man;
I'll objectify you if you don't mind.
I feel insecure, tra la,
Today, I'm a man.
I'll go off and invade a small country,
And no one will make any
Comments about the size of my penis.
I'm a man.

Today, I'm going to be a man;
I know what wines to order
I have good teeth! I'm a man!
I'm here! I'm large!
I like scotch and soda!
Women look at my finely boned hands, and swoon!
I protect the city from undesirables!
I own a really nice revolver!
I practise shooting
Imaginary diamond thieves over my desk!
I go to clubs and pick up cute young blonde women who giggle!
I'm a lawyer, I think!
Or am I a junior partner in my father's firm?
Or did I start my own software company
As a boy genius at eighteen, which now
Has subsidiary branches in New York, L.A.,
Munich, Paris and Berlin?
It's so hard to remember.

I'm a man today!
I'm so charming
You may want to hit me.
I have great cheekbones.
I'm sensitive, too,
I mean, overlooking that
Time I invaded the small country,
So they wouldn't think, you know...
But no, really,
I care about the environment, and things like that,
And I think it's important that
We all start paying attention to the world
Around us.
I love you.
Really.
You're one of the most caring,
Open women that I've ever met.
There's something about you

That's so ... so honest.
I worry about you, you know.
When you're not with me.
Let me see you home.
Waiter!
Thank you.
Ah.

When the light hits you like that, it's magical.
I don't want to keep you up too late...
No, that's fine, the weather's perfect,
It's only a short walk,
Well then, as long as you tell me when you want me to leave...
You don't have to be kind if you don't want to...
Lewis Carroll!
Yes!
I'm a huge fan!
Oh, I want to kiss you!
You're so beautiful.
Yes!
Yes!
YES!
YES!

Yes, today I'm a man.
I weep openly at the ballet!
I'm involved in regional politics!
I get money for grants, and scoff openly
At Reform Party toadies
Who call me a special interest group!
I know good restaurants!
I explain how women really think to unhappy male friends!
I rush through the streets like wild boar in the thickets,
Pink, prickly, tailored, and debonair,
Singing hoarsely to the four winds.
I'm a man, yes;
Today, I am a man!

when i am old & grey

When I am old and grey,
My skin loose on my face,
Too familiar for divorce,
Then narcissistic young men
In tight jeans and black leather
Won't look at me, and wish
My shirt was off.

When I am old and grey,
With eyes that squint, and still require
Three sets of gold-rimmed lenses,
Then sincere and well brought up young men
Will listen politely for a while,
And bring me tea.

When I am old and grey,
With elbows everywhere,
And tiny wisps of hair
Sticking out from under my hat,
Proud young lawyers in elevators
Will no longer square their shoulders carefully,
And slip their hands into the pockets
Of expensive pants when I get on.

When I am old and grey,
A wizened old bird,
I'll listen at keyholes,
Carry extra string,
And live on air.

only a profound thought can spawn a demon

written by death waits

*There is no knowledge ... We live in nothing but delusion
And still we are aquiver with anxiety that not even they will remain
— Vladimír Holan*

doctor's office

1.
the trendy, the important
what is commonly considered great
it is all inane beyond reason, beyond hope
beyond hype
like rumours that everybody hates you
and you will never be able to sell another poem
again...

at a party I am told
I look like someone who probably
thinks he's a genius
I admit it, it's true
I stand before you shamefaced over that particular grave
and some offices are like assembly lines
others like being welcomed into
a close friend's home
but more and more
all offices seem like laboratories of
man's inhumanity to man
waiting rooms
like graveyards for the terminally unamused
and accusations of this nature
like memoirs from the angst-filled rites of puberty
and beyond

and yet how simple it is for me to say
that it is all inane, every last drop
not to mention the exceptions
the vagaries and commitments of personal taste
to watch love stumble away
and not to cry out: *"wait,*
I take it all back
I don't care if you're inane
none of that matters now
we were destined to be together..."

2.
I went out drinking with my hand last night
for every drink I bought it
it promised to write me another glorious poem
a poem that would put it all to rest
a poem that would give birth to
a new kind of elation from the tissue of my head
(the implement of my ambition)
and let me breathe free again, sweet unbitter breaths
yes, mighty yes
I got my hand very drunk indeed that night
too drunk to perform for me
and I tossed and turned trying to sleep
all the while wondering if poetry was worth it
wondering why I didn't enjoy watching movies anymore
wondering if I was wrong
and they were right
and the strange elation could be found
through making money and dating women
or keeping an eye on the pop charts
rooting for the latest hit
the latest dream, the latest promptness:
just waiting to think something profound

32 – death waits

and actually realize it when it happens
if one is born a poet
one dies a moron
at the hands of the moment
at the hands of one's own poetry

3.
and really
more wild images, wilder images, please
more shotgun flying elephants and
colonized drug rings, imaginative rock star colonies
and bowling balls that roll south for the winter
people who think of civilization as a crime
against the planet
and others who think of the planet as an outmoded concept
soon to be done away with
dreams of tragic sexless love and the fragile irony
that is killing me, slowly, neatly, passionately
anyway
within the parameters of my carefully constructed persona
descriptions of machiavellian smiles and hairstyles
that eloquently define complex mathematical equations
more and more and even more
gangsters who build cities out of old celluloid
canisters and buildings that continue
to reshape themselves
long after the construction crews have left the site
songs about songs impossible to sing and songs about
singers who have overdosed on other songs
vacationers who write suicide notes on the backs
of their train ticket stubs
and mysterious figures who wave at you when you
just can't be bothered to wave back
wilder and wilder and stupider and stupider

more and more and poetry which is not considered very good
unless it reads brilliantly in translation
and currency that increases in value the longer
you manage to keep hold of it
these are the barstools
these are the watermelons
this is the logic that
makes great things modern and mediocre things
flower with the perfume of ineptitude
cake and chocolate and malice
and me
somebody more and somebody more and more
and more and me, me, me
somebody please
there are secret agents (extremely violent)
underneath the dolly-cart conspiring to kill me
of all people
but soon more and more and soon
soon we will find out that both killing and suicide
do not even exist, not even slightly
are no longer valid concepts
doctors talking about art
artists talking about profiteering
words are everywhere, yes
words are everywhere
the images are drowning
in life

on extremism

quiet retching, a fever that lasts my entire life
the inability to function, lethargy, seasoning
and when we expect children to fire guns
a catharsis which can only end with the electric lightbulb
a down-to-earthness which can only end the world

endless migraine headaches, i.e. the attraction to apocalypse
the reluctance to tell a story, modernity, action
and when my entire life becomes a medical experience
happiness, relief, a joyous lack of effort
bad poetry, writing for money, a lack of strength
and a lack of cash

just in case...

Just in case I wanted to write something
I carried all my possessions everywhere I roamed

For I could not write a poem about dying
without my library
And I could not write a poem
about the dark night of the human soul
without all my records
and a stereo on which to play them

So just in case I wanted to write something
I carried all my possessions everywhere I roamed

I could not write a poem about hope
without my washing machine
Any more than I could write a poem about
the need for spirituality
without my Maytag dishwasher

So just in case I wanted to write something
I carried all my possessions everywhere I roamed

There was no chance of writing a poem
about the French revolution
without a stove
and a pot full of pasta to cook on the front left burner
Just as there was no way I could write a poem
about love
without a thick stack of various
informative and trendy magazines

36 – death waits

So just in case I wanted to write something
I carried all my possessions everywhere I roamed

My back is sore and I have headaches often
I am sick of all this lugging about
But there is nothing I can do
nothing to do at all
for all the words I know
all the poetry I possess
and that possesses me
is etched deeply into the margins
of my material wealth

in a world that thirsts only for autobiographical detail

I set up a front
a double, a beard
to prevent connections from being made...
most days I don't think I'm going to make it
most days I'm wrong

They all sent out press releases
because that is the way it is done
thoughts about existence, about friendliness...
as is my lot in life
I am smothered by my creations

Every word seems the last
without some change, some revelation
some sense of arrival, the spirit of the times
a question mark becomes a heart attack
but candlelight is beautiful
even in an electrical storm

Karoshi: death from overwork

Heartbeat, tiny heartbeat
what's doing

Do you still crave success
or has exhaustion
stolen that from you as well

where is peacefulness?

I am carefully watching the sky
searching for some imperfection
and thinking about Pasolini
walking the streets of his death

He worked hard all his life
and then in heaven
he worked hard too
apologizing for all the hurt
he had inspired
just trying to get by

And if today I suffer
and tomorrow I don't suffer
or vice versa

or if today I work
and tomorrow I don't work

38 – death waits

at what moment might I realize
and not just realize
but truly know

that the goal is not
tomorrow, or next week, or next year
but right now, immediately

and then I ask myself
for truly I do not know

when does life begin?

# SLOP: an in-depth expose

hark
the sturdy movement of bicycle spokes approaches
screeching lessons, sturdy lessons
of how to fall in love with someone
who will never understand a word you are saying
yes yes, they squalk and advise
and then are gone like a mist
with the rest of the traffic

but still they approach
slowly, grisly
wait for them
their gears clatter in fifths
clattering above the traffic
but it's really their drivers we're staring at
as tears water and well up
upon the edges of the sewer grates
and fall in love with each other

falling in love with each other
that is the trick to it
with that part of yourself that adopts
the features of the other
with the way you feel about yourself
in the dwindling moments after orgasm
and if you can believe in that
then the phone rings
and you wonder if you should answer it

be my guest
the handle bars hold up entire castles of faith
drug dealers do their best to fill the sewers
with their own slop
under-tire mud splashes over curbs
and minute by minute they get closer
with a pound of the hammer
the strange ones pedal backwards
and get everywhere
yes, yes
we have amnesia here

and remember who all your lovers were
their faces, their bodies, their bicycles
all the drinks you bought each other
the liquids you cried and pissed
in each other's presence
and in the presence of others
backwards bicycles
will take you places good sex alone cannot

and hark
the wildly pedaling bicyclists approach
can you tell their names from their sprockets
I ask you, I ask you, I tell you
in this poem the bicycle represents
both the soul and the body
but never the face
never the face
never the face...
I'm sorry

flesh dress not health threat

The body ages
as others fade away young from hunger
and others paint blasphemy in colours
and yet others write words

and the paint awash in turpentine
swirls into the places of our lifestyle
and all the books written, so casually
spin round the world on thin speeding trains

and still the body ages…

"I was hungry once, that hungry, so I have some idea
what it's like…"
but how far might you need to travel
to truly know the stripes of that sensation?
one month? two months? five years? ten years?
or every single waking moment of your entire life
from the moment of birth to the moment of death
or maybe only one single Sunday afternoon
of scalding stomach cramps and constipated retching
as imagination leads you further from there
and you can truly know things
you have never felt

The body ages
as unseen bellies swell, not with child
but with some obscene parody of the opposite
and others are hooked up to reasonably comfortable machines
that might keep them alive forever

42 – death waits

which is one pillow-fluffing too long
for my tastes to swell:
flesh becomes meat
becomes shit becomes earth
and still the body ages...

The painter's back is bad and strains on the ladder
to stretch paintings bigger than the gallery walls
so as to move on to bigger galleries

The writer trusts his instincts so much he cannot even grasp
the simplest implications
of his own writings

The starving know nothing of politics
except for the ones who do
and even about those few
one cannot make generalizations

The elderly count the understated pennies
that will float them far past cognition
idling away in hospital beds
built more for machinery than for man
as the deaf die along with the screaming

and still the body ages...
and still the body ages...

Doors are painted on the sides of trucks
trucks that make deliveries
deliveries that are deliverances
as Jesus trods one more tired step
across the water

and books are written about everything
and books are written about everything
and books are written about everything
and yet more books are written about everything

yet still the body ages...
and still the body ages...

The doctors take their paycheques home in coffins
and I mean this as a metaphor
for why we attempt healing
and why we attempt anything
that is one last shot at eternity

The very young
first healthy and third sick alike
are all tuned into the same channel
(it's a channel where money equals life and
everything else equals suffering)
except for the exceptions
and who knows what they're thinking
hopefully not such thoughts as mine
as the mind remains lucid
and the body ages

and then once there was a wisp
a gleam in the eye of this elderly serenity
and this gleam, it short-circuited the world
and cost no one anything
and then it withered as I watched it
and it was so beautiful
so beautiful
and still the body ages...

the tragedy of change

what is good and what is bad   it won't last
long before the body crumbles in the earth   alive and fighting
a solution cannot be found   beyond the master and the cripple
and to rely on pain   or genius   or adaptability
forget it   it won't last

time speeds and bends   pretends to do the talking
but for every gain   a loss   and without gain
there is also loss   and without loss
a pain that is not a pain   a nothingness
a solution that is no solution
and even that will not last   it won't last

and I want   to make this perfectly clear
a world where everything   lasts forever
would be a world of dead stumps   but that doesn't
make the tragedy   any less tragic
and we are not even allowed tragedy today
forget it   take a valium   it won't last

towards a contentless society

it is content that abhors a vacuum
when the dove smacks into the wall
and in doing so is redeemed

content that cannot show its face within the storm
when the split second between stations
becomes the only time allowed for thought

and trying to write the saddest poem
humanity could possibly write
(but what would it contain?) a nothing,
a nothingness: evolutions definition of humanity

my heart is beating faster
than a thousand cracking whips
I bleed from every orifice
and not a single drop of blood
is sacred

give me survival

give me the writer who does
not wish to write anymore
the actor who does not want to act
the poet who has no use for poetry
the painter who puts down his brush
and goes back to school to study architecture
and I will show you
survival today

survival today is the denial
of humanity's true calling
it is pretending we are animals
and we are animals, wounded ones
so there is no reason to pretend
is there?

give me a language that
no longer wants to be spoken
a moment in history that
has been airbrushed out of the photograph forever
a sense of paranoia that
doesn't react when it is attacked
and I will show you
survival today

the church of the common cold

if we can agree that the basis for all religion
is the thesis that mankind is greater
than the sum of its parts
then I propose the church of the common cold
for what else do we share more completely
than the experience of stuffed-up noses
sneezing, coughing and sniffling

services would be held in winter only
a seasonal devotion
Kleenex boxes would line the pews
prayers would be chanted in a clogged, nasal unison
and fever would be the measurement
of one's inherent spiritual worth

for what else do we have in common anymore?
what illusions still stand, what civilized contrivances
can still bear the weight of our tender and sacred need
for hope?...
if I can hear myself sneeze
will it rattle the world?...

I am waiting for spring, when my spiritual practice
can restfully wither
and these jokes made at the expense of humanity
can stare at the sun
and be warmed

on his solitude

the owner of this establishment
does not crave community
not completely hollow, not completely
does not put daily the precepts of his existence
into question
does not have friends
does not ask questions
values money, values hard work
drinks cognac, coffee
addresses me by my first name
is happy to play a part in the advancement of culture
knows all these people as well
but doesn't hate them
doesn't fill up notebooks like they were going out of fashion
agrees with the shorter line lengths
goes to see every talented show
is a figment of my imagination
is standing right behind me
is bored with what he's reading
but not sick with it all
making a profit off my presence
in the restaurant around the corner
from the theatre

apricot pits

I was at the library
gawking at the hundreds of Canadian books
containing billions of Canadian poems
numbed by the size of our national literature
so instead of reading some
went home and ate an apricot
spit the pit into the garden
and tried desperately to think of some reason
any reason
why the world needed
another poem

while I was thinking
the apricot pit grew into a tree
in possession of meathooks
instead of blossoms
on each meathook hung a great, dead poet
wearing the clothing of my childhood
which did not fit them

I looked up at Blake and Holan,
Eliot and Celan, Valery and Wordsworth
and many more I have not yet read
and asked them
give me some advice
cheer me up a bit
but great poets were not put on earth

50 – death waits

to cheer up other younger poets
and I thought I'd rather have a tree
that grew apricots

suddenly all the poets began to speak at once
reciting their complete works
in loud, clear voices
and though each individual poem
was quite possibly beautiful
in its own right
I could barely make out more
than a phrase here and there
among the chaos,
the cacophony of this fruitless tree
was eating up all the nuances of great poetry
and with it our desire for great poetry
devoured as well

this is quite possibly the most Canadian poem
I have ever written
it must be all those uneven books
nobody ever withdraws anymore
nobody ever borrows from

five years ago I would have said
writing a poem about being Canadian
is even stupider
than writing a poem about nothing at all
but now I know better
the apricots taught me well when they said:

Canada is too cold a place for us to grow
instead you must grow dead poets

and that is what I did

written by Paul Howell McCafferty
photos by Stephanie Palmer

TEN THOUSAND LEAGUES UNDER THE SKULL

"That man is a dancer is an anachronism — Who has forgotten all his steps or hardly learnt them yet." — Louis MacNiece

i am a drum

I am a drum.
Not to all,
to some.
Strike me!
Softly,
hit
me.

Strum
at
my
belly.
The skins
of
my
eyes
are
soft
supple
waters.

From them
pulse
rhythms
from the sticks
of
my
brain.
No one
can say
what causes
my sound.
Skin or stick?

I am a drum.
Each sound
flees
the
resound
of
my
mouth.

I
am
beaten
constantly,
by
hands
of
friends
and
foes
alike.

The
easy
assonance
keeps
me
in
time.
Making
sure
my
tautness
is
in
accordance
to
their
rhyme.

Without
my
drummers
I am
mute.
The
quick
rhythmic
clicks
of
books.

The
heavy
honourable
hands
of
blinding
Poets.
The
high
rolling
beats
of
blinded
Priests.

All
send

rhythm,

out

as

I

send

this

to

you.

ten thousand leagues under the skull

Dancing with the endorphine dolphins,
green-bellied and laughter-eyed
In the high and happy sea of a morning ocean.
Turning with the fresh fins
through cool fantastic fathoms
on the smooth grooves and glass backs of future songs.

Hopping the helms of the seahorses,
head to the skinny surface.
Riding the ridding waves of sound
at sixty knots.
Up.
Face to face with the sugary sun.
Till a moment, plunging, bubbling,
back on seesaws of tidal tranquility.
Strashling past the cackling corals.

Whooshing, we sub-aquatic gods of frolic.
Gliding lovers in the curing chasms
of the borders of the caverns
at the corners of the soul.
Myself and the endorphine dolphins,
to the courts of the kings of the sea.

Dancing the sea star two-step.
There to swim endlessly.
A journey for all eternity
on the looping core of a rapture
that is the heart, the head,
the speaking spine of Neptune.
Throned and cloaked in the
soaking sanctuary of the exalted.

— for my mother and father

at the end of the dawn

At the end of the dawn, behind the tumbling sky lie the humblest of heavens where habit vows that all be stacked in multiples of seven. Behind me my friend, lies an almost you hairless, unhorsed fiery fermenter of faithless hope. Through the door that swings on art peeks a bleak suspicious shiny silence. POINT-BLANKLY-RED-WHITE-HOT-QUIET. Behind the hundred thousand serotonin selves that fence us in lies a soul,

infinitesimal
as
atom
speculum
of
clocks
lighthoused
on the
impulse
rock.
Cocooned
asleep
still
pulsing
in
another
time.
The
electric
vibrant
auroral
rhyme
silent
and
seeping,
ever
so softly
in a
quaint
and
quiet
violence.
Till
mouths
rupt
from
the
dowsing
tongue.
Flames
catch,
petrolled
in
instant
flood,
and
all
the
world's
a
fire
again
of
words.
Smoldering
like
the
first
one.
Raging
like
the
last.

the windmill

Stepping sodden from
blanket pelts of rain.
Lightly, she tossed her locks.
Spraying the white wood wall
in dots, tiny spits of water.
Taking my coat off
I handed her it
saying
"Dry your hair"
She turned around
"Can you get this?"
A red ribbon in her hair.

Moving toward her
still panting from
the recent rain break.
Cautious, tremoring in languor
I stooped
a soaking shamble,
to untie the wet
red knot.
It happened,
as far as I recall
like the rain.

Tremulous
Giddy paced and dumb
with passion,
we kissed in a hectic tumble.
Awkward and ecstatic
in the first jolty commotion of love.
Hitching at clothing
like farmers at hay
or agitated folk in phosphorus.

The sawdust was smooth
as we dreamt of who we were.
Flushed as apples
on the windmill's floor.

After the act
I remembered my moaning
restrained and residual
in the echoed mount of the mill.
I remember how darkness fell
as if huddling our secret closer
and a cold tingle bit my toes
as she slept on my chest.

I remember her waking
asking in a cute curious puzzle
why I was weeping.
I remember my laughing
faint
hollowed out against the
falling rice of the rain and
her voice
"You won't forget me, will you?"

Nine years later now
I remember this.
A dark figure
silhouetted
on a hill,
I stand here.
Again.
As a red rag
tied to a sail
ruffles.
A voice keeps repeating
"Why do you weep?"

miss
— for Zoie

Your form is propitious to us all,
like a thrown back divan
or the easy smoothness
of an invariable liquid —
Selfless Harmony.
Or the most comfortable
dip of an easy armchair.
Staired to those
pillars of sky,
running with translucent
angel tears.
Tasters from sparkling legends
that clean the hunched and
harbour bodied Gods,
holding frozen romans of thought.
I tend to tune in on you
on half-asleep
DIRKY-NEAR-LIGHT-NEAR-MISSED,
mornings.
Stamped out and posted with loneliness,
large coffee booked words
and laced with the legs
of the leftover dances
from later day clouds.

betty blue

Sometimes, I get feelings.
Or a feeling that
Beatrice Dalle's mouth is
Ahh!
Ohhh!
Ummm!
A voluptuous
flowering
inferno
of soft
volcano.
And I want to
is
Ohhh!
Are
Ahhh!
The
Ayyess!!
Are
Ahh!
Lips
Like
Bleeding
Sucking
Tasting
Roses!
Ohh!
Erupting like a dance
In a Parisian cave.
Ahh
Is
Are
Sweet Jesus!!!
Crossed
Bless'd
And
slightly
undressed.

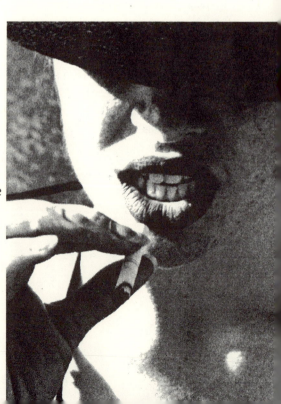

the bird disease

My lover lay sleeping
I heard a fluttering.
It was the white flightless
bird of her unspoken words.

My brother sits staring.
I hear a screeching.
It is the dark bird of prey
of his unspoken ways.

My friend sits thinking
two thousand miles away.
I hear strange caws
see veiny blues
dark wine reds.
It's the birds of paradise
that sing inside his head.

My soul stops singing.
Halts to a claptrap.
Declares itself nothing.
Twit - twoos twice
and flies off.
My lover's bird
in its mouth
dead
limp and
dripping
with
beautiful poetry
that splats
fat splods
on all
below.

Infecting them with
this

incredible

plague

now

creeping

down

my

page.

housecall

I don't quite feel myself.
It's odd to feel this way.
I've tried six times already,
sixteen times yesterday.
Oh! What the hell is wrong with me.
I don't mean what I say.

My hands are raw this morning.
My words just won't obey.
Oh! send for Doctor metaphor
and Sister simile.

Oh, send for Doctor metaphor
to help my words get bigger.
With sexy Sister simile
to soothe me with her figure.

My words fell out the window.
They're in my arms, still bleeding.
Please, please! Don't let them
die on me, they're fading and receding.

Oh, where is Doctor metaphor
his case full 'O' comparison.
What's this? Sister simile's
run off with Shakespeare
on a marathon?

Huh, typical!!

Come, hurry quick!
I'm floundering!
My alphabet can't breathe.
Oh, Doctor please! Stroll up
the path with something to relieve.

Too late.
All's lost, I'm losing them.
My words are all flatlining
and the Doctor's voice at the
end of the line, says,
"I'm at Di Vinci's Restaurant,
with Leonard Cohen,
dining."

a kinda gettin' down thang

— for Chris Allan

There's funk in the fridge
it's so groovy.
There's funk in the fridge
and in the hall.
There's two blind mice
building discos in the rice
and a parrot gettin' ready
for a ball.

There's two dumb beats
in the biscuits,
three snare drums
in the tea.
There's funk in the cream
in the coffee,
with a base that heats
the water up for me.

There were songs in the
hair of Albert Einstein
high moves in the chalk
that MC^2

There's a big, big sky
with a twinkle in its eye.
A dance that's hangin'
groovy in the air.

There's the old, sad sailor
by the cafe.
With tambourines dug
deep inside his heart.

There's an instrumental
smoothness to the ocean
that bore his body back
here to the start.

There's a soul of a sad
lover in his kitchen
dripping from the taps
in constant longing.

There's a word for
the birds and the
music that we've
heard.
It's not culture,
not creation,
it's belonging.

yukon store

Adrift on a grey October
ocean
eyes so cold,
frozen
to
the
corneas
by the
weather
that
the
alphabet
forgot.
Out
by
glaciers
of
words
wormed
together
in
numb
institutions
of
iced
Sunday
whiteness.
Snowy
blank,
steely
and
cutting
my
ankles
on
the
passing
like
huge
rare
razor-
backed
hacksaws.
Too big,
too cold
and
far
too
hard
to
break
even
a
mouse-
eyed
shard.
Not
the
slighty
atom
of a
sentence
nor
the
faintest
glimmer
of
a
distant
verse.
Nothing.

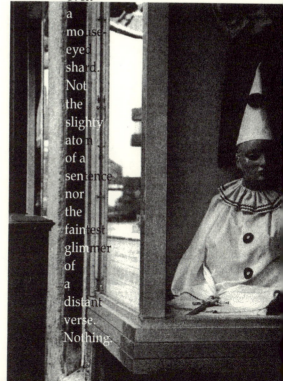

Nobody
came.
All
clear
the
ocean.

The
mild
semiconscious
mine
of
brain.

Overdosed
on
the king of soul
and
heaps
of
powders.

Had
wiped out
connection
communion
or
should
I
say
communication
was
blasted
unaware
like
Titanic
tourists
with
their
pants
down.

Then?
up
popped
this
submarine

surfacing

slowly

in

your

deepest

head.

where's the paisley pattern now?

— *for Michael Quail*

Shhh!

Children are sleeping.
The future is dreaming them.
All over the city
black dogs are waking
yawning
stretching
and
haunching
to
howl.

Shhh!

The clouds
peel
like
bedsheets
for Mummy Moon
proud
in
a
round
yellow
maternal
smile.

The streets
are
thick
with
loneliness
like
GOO
STICK
PAINT
TAR!
Creaky
doors
are
being
opened.
Nearby
in
hallways
coats
are
being
dropped.
There
is
sighing
from
children
still
awake.

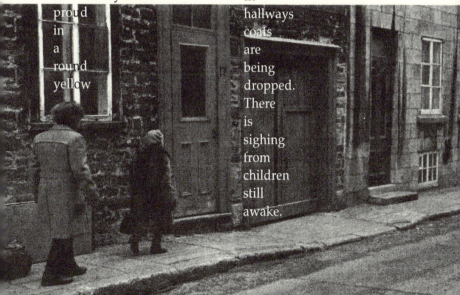

Home
from
work.

Matches are struck,
cigarettes are lit;
blazing
thimble
sticks
to
ward
off
meeting
something
scary,
like
themselves!

Shhh!

Feet are tabled.
Lids lower
for
liftoffs.
Mother
is
clothed.
She
keeps
an
eye
elsewhere.
Here and there,
hands
are
being
held.
Words
like
scattered
flocks
of
soft
rare
flowers
are
tiny
golden
flecks
pinnied
on
the
painted
pain
of
night.

Shhh!

Mouths
are
dreaming
the
future.
Dogs
begin
to
settle.
The
message
is
quite
clear.

autumn

Autumn's guest is a new patience
coolly, crisply, correctly and evenly
a slow tide of overturning rest,
a new clairvoyant clarity,
strewn amongst the littered leftovers
of summer's ousted feast.
The barren nakedness of honest trees,
their stripet shadings
clearly lain out
in unrelenting rows
of lengthy decoration.
Leaves are not gold,
they are bronzy, copper, yellowed,
crumpling with the crinchy
starchy, fertile voice of tomorrow.
A place utterly worn out,
laid wide open
like an old fellow
telling the bundles
of a life, gathered in heaps of
riper wisdom.
Emptying from it
all that was lost in a gaunt silence,
an eerie shade.
When he was young
there was no time to talk.
No time to tell.
Being young and strident
cloaked him in his vaulting youth
like the forest on a midsummer night,
darting in amongst itself.
Quick flashing covenants
of giggling green
small trotting battalions of elfish flowers.

Tying itself up in a secret
as binding, as un-fathomnable as time itself.
Ticking in the un-mouthable montage
of snakey trees.
Dumb gloved grasping giants,
heaving at roots
as eager children at
"STAY THERE!"
chairs.
This Autumn Palace
like the man
is cleared, bright, lined
and scrawny aged
in the etchings of its sky-
strickling hands.
Its brown, breathing,
brilliant book,
dives again,
into the deep burrowed fathoms
of forever.
Exploring without question,
its own world,
its billion
un re-retellable Bibles
before raising again
its massive cry,
lullabying self,
A gooing and gurgling
for the millionth time,
a two-headed creature.

One offering breast.
The other open mouthed.

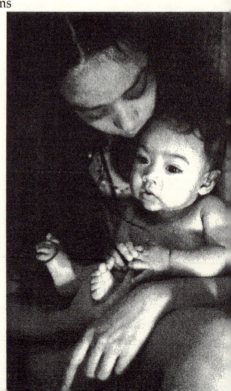

a home so far it's nowhere but memory

Diana Fitzgerald Bryden

Breakfast on the Queen Car

This morning on the Queen streetcar
I knew that it was summer.
The seat in front of me was taken
by a man whose soft curly black hair
was thinning a little, along the part,
and in that spot his scalp was so white,
so tender-looking,
I wanted to lay my finger there
and stroke
up and down, up and down.
I knew if I did he would purr like a cat,
turn and lick me all over my face
with his hot thick rough tongue.

That sweet furrow tempted me
all the way from Dufferin to Shaw.
I couldn't hold back (it must be the weather),
I had such a yearning, such a thirst,
that after my finger, I laid there
my own tongue, smooth and wet.
I licked up and down
and his scalp turned soft.
It opened
to spill his sweet white milk.
I opened him up with my greedy tongue,
opened his head and tasted his spirit.
His wet thoughts spilled down my throat
as he laid his head back
the better to feed me.

At Bathurst, when I got off for work,
he pressed himself shut and waved me goodbye
and we thanked each other for breakfast.

The fish

You caught that fish like a good fast fuck,
all wet and fishy, all finger sticky.
Gloved in fluids, you tried to unhook him.
Torn by the hook, the fish was sick.
He coughed and shook like a sick old smoker,
he gagged and choked
and you tried to stroke the hook out
but its bright point
sat deep in the wet,
deep in the flesh.
Go deep in my flesh, love, and I'll hold on tight.
I'll loosen when the brightness comes whirring
out of the flesh, shivering and spinning.
Help me, you're calling, *help me hold him!*
The fish in my arms is a desperate baby,
his eyes are wet peas
crinkled and cloudy,
milky with pain.
Milk in the flesh.
He writhes like a baby
and blood spills like urine
in ribbons, in streamers.
He swells in my arms
Till I'm up to the elbows
in fish blood and water.
You can't free the hook,
he thrashes and wrestles,
you bite through the line and he leaps for the water,
trailing behind him a thick spool of whiteness,
the hook still inside him,
the two of us soaked,
hands raw from wetness, cheeks smeared with wetness.
Dig deep my fisherman,
I'll pull you in.

notes for a love poem

I could be the hand in your pocket,
carelessly kept, impossible to part with.

Beside you in sleep,
I'd know all your secrets.
And at table,
curled round your knife,
I'd feed you.
For you I'd be capable,
dexterous, steady. Cold when you are,
and hot. Easy to love,
easy as instinct, and no matter what
you forgot or left behind
it wouldn't be me. (I'd never leave —
where could I go without you?)
I'd be nervous when you were, or ready,
I'd help you get dressed, or, better yet, caress
yourself. But wait —

Would I have to die with you,
or at least be still,
if you said so?
Get up, go to bed
according to your whims?
Switch off the light
when I wanted to read,
go out at night
when I was tired?
And as your hand, would I have to be there
when you stroked other women?
(Or could I pinch them, instead,
and spoil your seductions?)

Wait! I've changed my mind.
Forget me living in your pocket,
I want you in mine.

Sappho's Rope

*...she hanged herself with
a rope made from the torn hems of
dresses.* Distracted from
a life by the beauty of its death.
Limp dresses, a hanging rope.

*Poetess of love in antiquity,
stand with me in my conflict.*
Honour me, watch
while I knot an O, a window
from my father's house.
Twisting lilies
into my quilt, a history plainer
than the ones
stitched by my patient sisters.

Dresses, unhemmed, hang
in my closet, unblown flags.
Danger. High wind.
This muscled rope
is all that's left. I asked
a question, now
close my eyes
on the answer. Stand with me
while I say goodbye.
No place for me here.

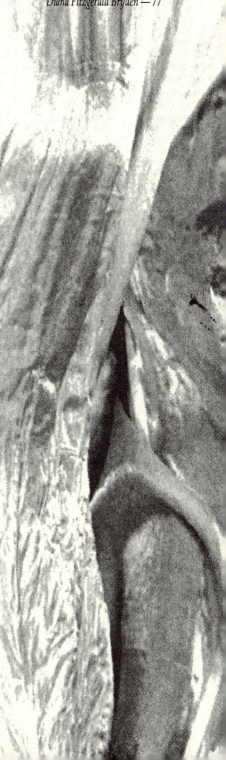

Portrait of Catherine Parr

I kept my head with Henry.
I fed him cream and port
till his feet puffed up like fat pincushions
and all he could think of was my sly comforts.
He wasn't his bloody self by then —
I had nothing to fear, really —
but still he was a lot of work.
You have no idea!

Now I do what I like:
ride my bicycle, take the bus,
eat lemons, tickle my puss,
sun my ankles by the swimming pool,
with nothing to fear, nothing to fear.

I still feel sorry for Mary.
That bitchy Anne could never bear
to see her have any fun,
and how Mary suffered.
Well, Anne suffered too, of course.
She was always a bit of a fool, as well as a bitch,
fussing over her bikini wax
or whether her thighs were too fat,
telling little Liza to run off and play —
Mummy's busy, Lizzie, go away —
but in the end I can't say she deserved
that big red wallop under her chin.

Many's the night I've sat
with my dear friend Lady Julia Roberts,
in front of the TV
or at the card-table, playing hearts,
and we've gone over it all,
all the blood and love affairs.

Such a shame! says Lady Julia,
as she fiddles with the antenna.
*And those poor girls, both of them —
Kate, where's the vodka?*
She's a great vodka-lover, is Julia,
as am I.

It gets my goat that Henry,
with his temper and his king-size appetites,
is so easy to remember,
while the rest of us get stuck on his key-chain.
I bet you can't even name us in order,
what with the state of formal education as it is.
Nor do you know that I have wondrous small feet.
Or that silly Anne was always late,
rushing to-and-fro
the Estée Lauder Beauty Palace,
doing her Jane Fonda.

Jane was none too bright herself,
all her life she was a chronic giggler,
especially around men.
Not that she had much to giggle about, poor thing.
The other Anne was a nervous wreck,
she took pills to survive
and to make her sleep.
Kate-in-the-middle was bookish
(she wrote poetry and walked in *her* sleep),
while the first Catherine lacked even a teaspoon of humour.
But she had her pride,
and I wouldn't be surprised
if it was her who started the rumours
that got Anne's head tipped from her shoulders.

Now that I look back
I can see that it's hard to keep track
of all the little details, even for me.
Still, you get the snapshot.
And as Lady Julia always says:
No press is better than bad press, Kate.
She's not kidding.

Anyway: this here is my best pearl headdress,
the one I gave to Mary
when I could see she would always suffer,
moping as she did, telling secrets to her pets,
pining for her Daddy's love.

And if you look carefully at this fine portrait, you can spy
that I'm wearing my ring, the one with the secret inscription.
No, you can't read it! It's a secret.

Lullaby

Late at night, a summer night,
drinking up the air like water
away from the brick-hot pit
of my small apartment,
the sucked-up spat-out heat
of my apartment,
I sat at midnight in the park
with a pregnant woman as she brushed her hair.

The swings are newly painted purple,
an ether of purple above the metal,
tinting the air with a mist of colour, as if
no form could hold
in this softness,
all edges must dissolve.

Pale and small and pregnant
she lets her pale arms float,
brushing a lullaby through her hair,
rocking the cradle.

Sweeping a lullaby through her hair,
rocking the cradle.

She lets her hair
spill over her fingers,
its cool weight slip
through her hands like flowers.

Brushing a lullaby through her hair,
rocking the cradle.

Sweeping a lullaby through her hair,
rocking the cradle.

We sit for an hour in the quiet rhythm.
We could fall asleep in a bed of purple,
wake in the cool morning
and like children walk home.

Theft

She walks outside; stone is water, flowing
away from memory. She hears sirens
crying. Set loose, severed
from the ribbons of sight.

Eighty years ago, helping her father
deliver the laundry, she waits with the horses.
His seat beside her, emptied
of him, holds his warmth.
She falls asleep
breathing leather and animal.

I steal small mouthfuls,
a rude bird, snatching from her: *sheets and towels,
stone-white cotton.*

A thief, I fly through the maze
of her memory; dead ends
and tunnels diverging
from my purpose: to feed my hunger, but also
to replace lost sight — comfort
with words. Break the stillness
with a sudden flicker
of light, or another small theft.

*I was so tiny, I could stand
underneath the horses.
Or they were so big. My head
barely touched their bellies.*

Yellow

for Genie

Taught to speak at the age of 13,
having been confined by her father until then.

An aperture
in the darkness, yellow.
An edge
of blue, biting through
the window like a hungry mouth,
hungry for anything
but the food he gives me.

Yellow has a voice, not like the grey
of his, but a voice as soft
as the arms of someone who
might hold me, tender and amused.
So much to laugh at!
His long face, his bitter breath
as he lifts me
off the stained pot. Instead
of girlish frills
around my dress, a ruffle
of flesh, calloused
from the seat
I'm locked to, day in
day out. Outside,
the dog sings
on his chain,
the two of us sing.

And this is not my voice, this poem
that you're reading,
no one knows
the true colour of my voice.

Except, now that I'm
away from him,
strangers arrested
by its echo: a woman
who stopped me
on the street, ran from her car — the music
of change hitting vinyl seats — thrust
her small red plastic purse
at me, said "Let me
give you this. Take it, honey."
Her kindness soft
as green.
The man in the store who,
having watched me walk through
the aisles with Jean,
left a bead necklace
for me at the cash.

What trail of colour
follows me
like a bright hem, pulling
in its wake green,
yellow, blue?
Colours, that
these doctors
are deaf to, hard as they listen
for some coherent sound (pressured
to give the experiment of my life
some real
value in their world) — some sign
that their work
has been rewarded — a sign
that won't be found, or not by them.

Colour started in that pale
house where my father met the dark
at night with a shotgun in his lap.

His red and grey the only words
other than the quiet mouths
of blue and yellow,
whose small comforts, their small
warm noise, I took
and kept for my own voice,
though in the end I am
too quiet, for most who try,
to hear.

Sick house

Next door is a poison house.
It's sick, and it sticks its yellow tongue out
at anyone who hears
the sad living that goes on there.
The parents fight, their two boys cry
and fight with each other,
and I sit by
stuck to the wall
through which their noise is seeping, seeping.
I turn small while I listen,
a five-year-old girl, and I make myself smaller,
unable to leave them.

I'm bound to those sorry wranglers,
splashed by the heat of their terrible quarrel,
a quarrel so old and everlasting
they're damned if they'll give it up.
They're making it into a perfect soup
that simmers,
intensifying its flavour,
giving off its poisons.

Now the front door opens, the boys tear out.
Out of the house like dogs after meat,
they run into the free air of the street to play hockey.
They bite at the air and growl at each other,
jumping like puppies in the summer weather,
wild as puppies at their release.

The father's escape is more discreet,
but just as eager.
He drives off in his car,
panting to get to his big-dog friends.
First he'll stop in the bakery,
and wag his tail at all the waitresses,
reminding himself that he *is* a big dog,

yes he *is* a big dog,
after all.

The mother, in everyone's books,
is captain cook —
she can't leave her job,
she must stir the pot,
and she has no wild skin to change into.
But she does get as far as the back garden.
Kneeling there now, fixing her plants,
her face is still fierce and raw —
her mouth a small lock on its shut door —
her hands are sure in their purpose
and her body, though it rejects all else
leans into the green, supple
and softening.

Inside Toledo

Abandonment. Inside the storm.
Light fractures; plates split
apart, gash the sky, spill cloud
and light. The earth
vibrates. No one crosses
the bridge. Green water. Reeds shiver; send ripples
of restlessness. Goosebumps.

The church, a bony finger,
points, warning, to the sky.
Metallic haze. Colour: bronze
and grey. Clouds rushing fields darken
the grass; dipped in shadow like hair in water.
We taste ozone. Throw windows open, feel the chill,
the storm's wet breath.

Far from home, surrounded
by travellers, neither alone
nor with friends. Pulled inside
Toledo, here in London. Waiting
for myself to return.

Vapour

Dreaming the city. Chipped basalt,
a wall. A gap in the wall —
six domes, unripe green stained gold.
A door, a promise that
shivers when you approach it.

Recognition: our closeness to
spirits, surviving the dead. Pressed
up against us. Breathing the past into
the present as they bend to kiss
stone floors; suck air
from concrete. Like breakfast-eaters at Pompeii,
tongues stilled by ash
or lemon vapour.

A father crushes his daughter's head in the rush
for the ceiling, she's slippery as
wet stone. In an open yard
candy showers glitter, a joke or
a mistake, handfuls studding
cold sand. A mother throws
her baby into the street; shouts a message
to her neighbours, then jumps

From the bakery we watch spring rain making
beaded shawls from wet hair, slick blossoms from
umbrellas. Our children's crankiness slips away, washed
under by rain.

Waiters bring coffee in bowls, smoky
with steamed milk. Silver blades shimmer
and snap in unison, slicing bread
for our table. Star-shaped cakes
under glass, on display
for my daughter.

We peel back time's skin
to find them, our ancestors
cheek-to-cheek with us, mouths open —
a blue kiss.

The Prizewinner

In a dry room
all dust and grey,
a small crowd waits
for what I'll say
next, which way I'll lead them.
I can feel the net
twisting
in their hands, the listeners,
as they strain to pull me in.

Me: the big man
whose body sags
from age and fatigue and from the weight
of holding up my own prestige;
the unexpected weight of words
that keep sufferers alive,
miles away — they tell me
in their letters. My poetry,
like a movie actor's familiarity,
like Harrison Ford's handsome face,
makes them think
they know me. They do, I guess,
but only for the time it takes
to write a poem.

Tonight I'm fishing
this crowd for something
that will move me: an invitation.
I'm tired, and this is the wrong place
to be — far from home,
from a home that's so far
it's nowhere but memory,
and my memory's
faulty. It twists
away from me like wet rope, burning my hands.
Burning me, as I try

to remember why
these blind
faces are turned to me; which prizes
I've won and
why they matter, how
I'll get back
to the work that is my only peace,
the only rest
I've earned, or kept.

I'm old enough now that
in spite of where I stand
the look I want from a woman
is no certainty, not
any more. Still it usually happens.
I can't be sure it will, but it usually does.
And then my sick starveling boy
falls on her breast and I forget
how far I've come,
what I've lost — my regrets
and the fact that no one
now comes close to me
without needing, wanting
or fearing something.
This nervous, angry boy, my youth,
sneers, is appalled
by what I am, a grand old man.

But I'm tired, and weariness
makes the noise
around me worse.
I'll feel better back in Boston,
but it's still not home, now
I've gone too far
to ever come home.

Song for a dead actor

Little brother, little lover,
when they lifted the top of your skull
what secrets slipped out?
Pale eyelids, sweet ripple
bone, flesh,
brightness.
Death spills over.
Beautiful boy, shining brother,
lord of a thousand and one love poems.
For you
girls and boys
sing songs of mourning.
On a sidewalk you slip down down
down in one long shudder.
No bloody car seats, but
a meadow
a small hand
static shivers
sleep
skin so fine, so delicate
a bad night leaves bruises.
His kindness shamed me.
We fucked in the park,
falling
in the sweet ripe grass.
I looked up at the sky.
Many small cruelties inflicted,
none of them by him.
Lord of a thousand nights,
to all troubled children
promise gentleness
wet
tangled
hollow
from your head spill
soft rain.

Other titles from Insomniac Press:

Playing in the Asphalt Garden
by Phlip Arima, Jill Battson, Tatiana Freire-Lizama and Stan Rogal

This book features new Canadian urban writers, who express the urban experience — not the city of buildings and streets, but as a concentration of human experience, where a rapid and voluminous exchange of ideas, messages, power and beliefs takes place.

The book is divided into four sections features each of the writers' works with unique graphic design, illustration and photography. Jill Battson's poetry leads the reader through the gritty streets of the city. Philip Arima's poetry shows a city of addiction and madness in all of its forms. Stan Rogal's short fiction reflects the complexity of control, identity and desire in relationships. Tatiana Freire-Lizama's writing depicts the longing and pride of immigrants looking back at where they came from.

5 3/4" x 9" • 128 pages • trade paperback • isbn 1-895837-20-0 • $14.99

Mad Angels and Amphetamines
by Nik Beat, Mary Elizabeth Grace, Noah Leznoff and Matthew Remski

A collection by four emerging Canadian writers and three graphic designers. In this book, design is an integral part of the prose and poetry. Each writer collaborated with a designer so that the graphic design is an interpretation of the writer's works. Nik Beat's lyrical and unpretentious poetry; Noah Leznoff's darkly humourous prose and narrative poetic cycles; Mary Elizabeth Grace's Celtic dialogues and mystical images; and Matthew Remski's medieval symbols and surrealistic style of story; this is the mixture of styles that weave together in *Mad Angels and Amphetamines*.

6" x 9" • 96 pages • trade paperback • isbn 1-895837-14-6 • $12.95

Insomniac Press • 378 Delaware Ave. • Toronto, ON, Canada • M6H 2T8
phone: (416) 538-4308 • fax: (416) 596-6743